For dogs everywhere and the people who love them

VINCENT

🕊 ALADDIN | An imprint of Simon & Schuster Children's Publishing Division | 1230 Avenue of the Americas, New York, New York 10020 | First Aladdin hardcover edition May 2020 | Copyright © 2020 by Terry Brodner | All rights reserved, including the right of reproduction in whole or in part in any form. | ALADDIN and related logo are registered trademarks of Simon & Schuster, Inc. | For information about special discounts for bulk purchases, please contact Simon & Schuster Special Sales at 1-866-506-1949 or business@simonandschuster.com. | The Simon & Schuster Speakers Bureau can bring authors to your live event. For more information or to book an event contact the Simon & Schuster Speakers Bureau at 1-866-248-3049 or visit our website at www.simonspeakers.com. | Book designed by Karin Paprocki | The illustrations for this book were rendered in pencil, pen, and ink on watercolor paper with digital coloring and photographic elements. | The text of this book was set in Bodoni Standard Book. | Manufactured in China 0220 SCP | 2 4 6 8 10 9 7 5 3 1 | Library of Congress Control Number 2019946556 | ISBN 978-1-5344-1356-6 (hc) | ISBN 978-1-5344-1357-3 (eBook)

V

Vinny lived with his mom and his adopted brother, Lester, a cat.

Every morning Mom would put on nice clothes and leave the house.

"Where does Mom go all day?" Vinny asked Lester one sunny afternoon.

"She has a job," Lester answered.

"What's a job?" Vinny asked.

Lester explained, "A job is a place where you do things for other people, and then they give you food and toys."

"Wow! I should get a job!" said Vinny.

"Don't be silly," replied Lester. "Dogs don't get jobs."

But Vinny was determined.

The next morning after Mom left for work, he put on his best suit . . .

and marched out the front door and down the street.

Soon Vinny saw a restaurant with a HELP WANTED sign on the door.

"Hello," Vinny said to a lady behind the counter. "I'm looking for a job."

"Great," said the lady. "Can you clean tables?"

"Of course," said Vinny.

The lady gave him an apron, and he waited for someone to leave a table.

Finally, he had a chance to show how well he could clean.

Immediately, Vinny hopped up onto the table and started licking the plates.

There was a lot of delicious tomato sauce and crumbs. Vinny thought he had found the perfect job.

"No, no, no!" the lady shouted.
"I didn't realize you were a dog! We don't hire dogs."

Vinny was confused, but he wanted a job and wasn't going to give up.

He saw another store with a HELP WANTED sign in the window.

Inside were leafy green plants from floor to ceiling as far back as the eye could see.

"Hello," Vinny said to the man behind the counter. "I'm looking for a job."

"Great," said the man. "We need someone to water the plants."

Vinny was very experienced at this and was eager to show how well he could do it.

Without being asked,
he began to water the plants.

"STO-O-O-OP!" cried the man in astonishment. "You are a dog, and we don't hire dogs!"

Vinny left, feeling very disappointed.

He had just about given up on getting a job when
he noticed a giant building with columns.

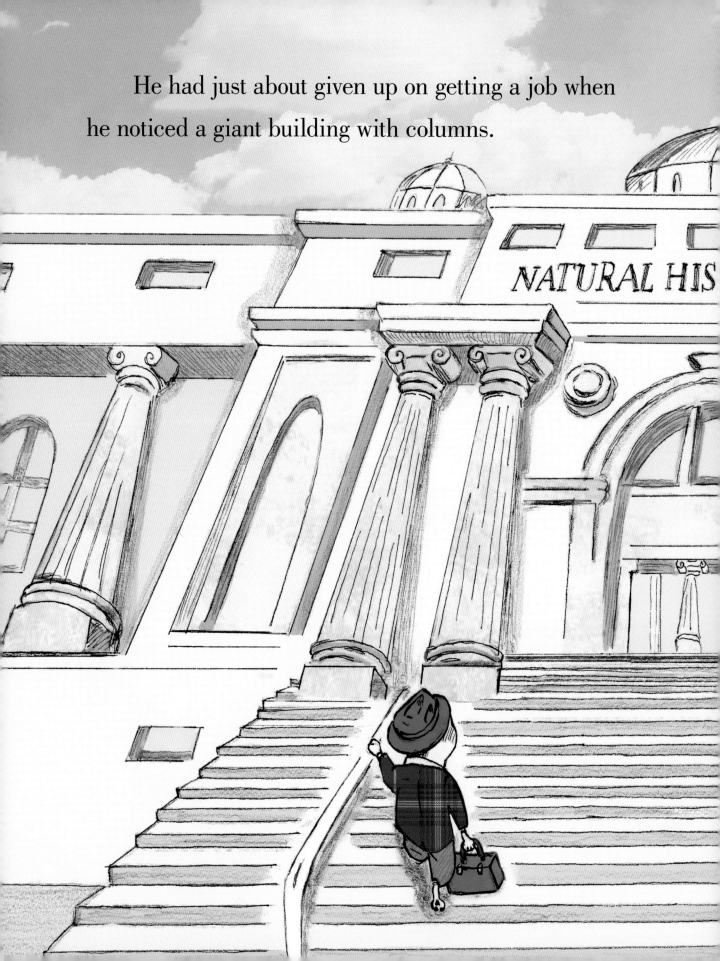

In a building that huge, he was sure extra workers were needed.

"Hello," Vinny said to the museum guide.
"I'm looking for a job!"

"Follow me," said the man, and they walked
into a great hall with the biggest collection of
bones Vinny had ever seen.

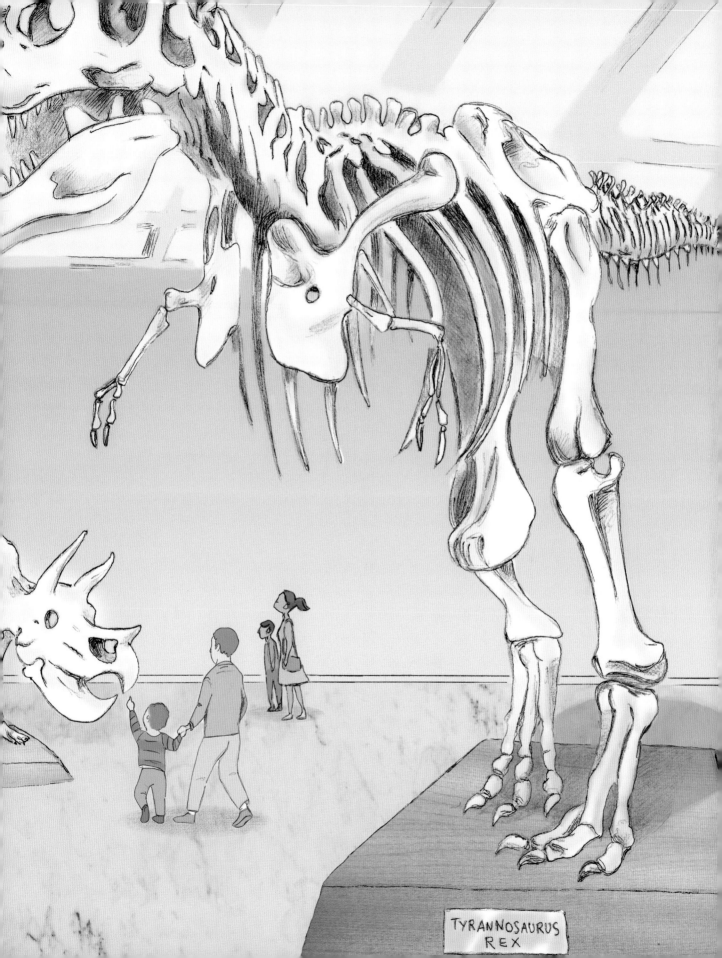

TYRANNOSAURUS
REX

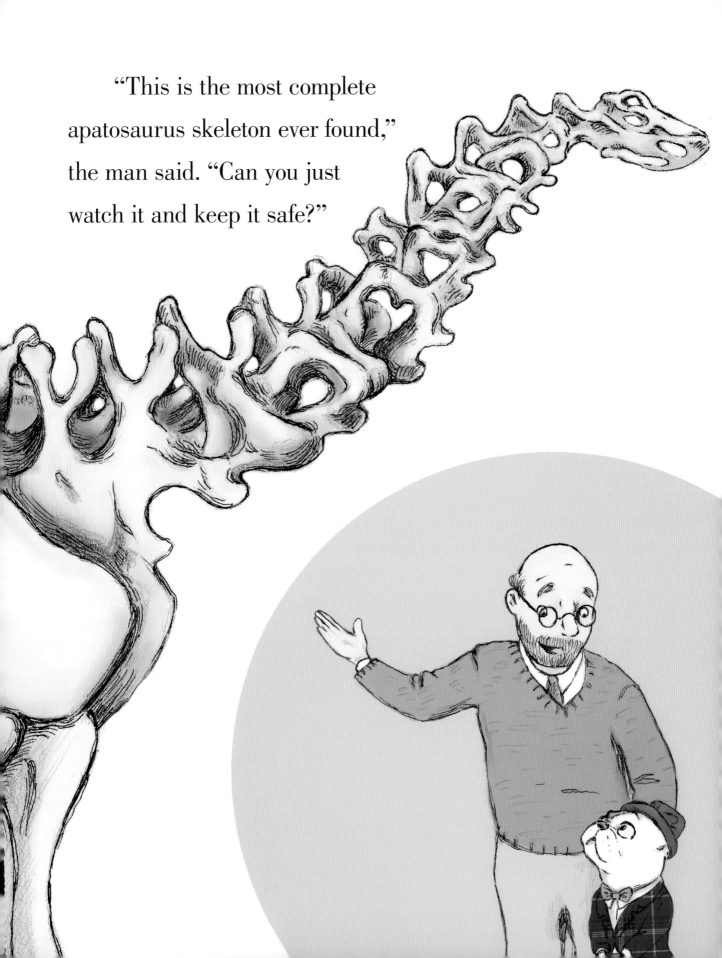

"This is the most complete apatosaurus skeleton ever found," the man said. "Can you just watch it and keep it safe?"

YES!

So Vinny watched the bones, and watched them, and watched them.

The more he watched them, the more delicious they looked!

No one would notice if I took a tiny bone, he thought. *They have so many here.*

He made sure no one was near, and gave a firm tug on the skinniest leg bone he could clamp his jaws on.

This might be harder than I thought.

He gave another yank, and another, until he heard a sharp POP!

He did it! He looked down at the bone and smiled. Just then, a loud rumble filled the room. The rest of the bones were moving!

Oh dear, thought Vinny, and . . .

he ran as fast as he could out of the museum and
all the way home.

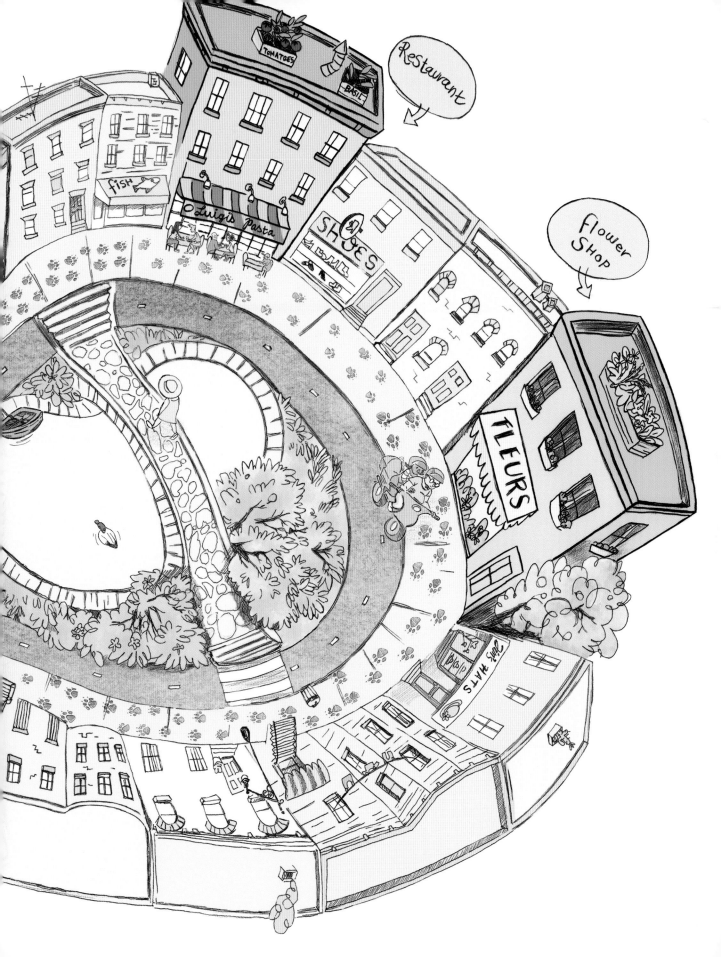

Mom was waiting for him when he got home.
"Where were you?! You had us worried sick!"
"Oh, I was just looking for a job like yours,
Mom, but I'm no good at jobs," said Vinny.

"You certainly are." Mom smiled. "You already have a job, and you are very good at it! You wake me up every morning, greet me when I come home, keep me safe, and love me all the time," she said, giving Vinny a big hug. "It's the perfect job for you—you're a dog!"

Meanwhile, at the museum . . .

"This *used* to be the most complete apatosaurus skeleton around," said the museum guide to a group of people standing around the dinosaur.

"Where'd its leg bone go?" someone asked.

APATOSAURUS

"We have no idea."
The museum guide sighed.